The frog landed smack on Ms. Barr's shoulder. She shrieked as it slid under her collar and down her back. She reached for it. But it had slid so far down that it was trapped at her beltline. Ms. Barr did a wild, twisting dance. She screamed and shrieked as the slippery bullfrog wriggled inside her blouse.

BIG CHAPTER BOOKS

The Berenstain Bears and the Drug Free Zone

The Berenstain Bears and the New Girl in Town

The Berenstain Bears Gotta Dance!

The Berenstain Bears and the Nerdy Nephew

The Berenstain Bears Accept No Substitutes

The Berenstain Bears and the Female Fullback

The Berenstain Bears and the Red-Handed Thief

The Berenstain Bears
    and the Wheelchair Commando

Coming soon

The Berenstain Bears and the School Scandal Sheet

The Berenstain Bears at Camp Crush

The Berenstain Bears and the Galloping Ghost

The Berenstain Bears
ACCEPT NO SUBSTITUTES

by Stan & Jan Berenstain

A BIG CHAPTER BOOK™

Random House 🏠 New York

Library of Congress Cataloging-in-Publication Data
Berenstain, Stan.
The Berenstain Bears accept no substitutes /
by Stan and Jan Berenstain.
   p.   cm. — (A Big chapter book)
SUMMARY: When a new substitute teacher comes to Bear Country
School, the cubs learn that appearances can be deceiving.
ISBN 0-679-84035-4 (pbk.) — ISBN 0-679-94035-9 (lib. bdg.)
[1. Schools—Fiction.   2. Bears—Fiction.
3. Conduct of life—Fiction.]   I. Berenstain, Jan.   II. Title.
III. Title: Accept no substitutes.   IV. Series: Berenstain, Stan.
Big chapter book.
PZ7.B4483Beag 1993   [E]—dc20   93-8869

Manufactured in the United States of America   10 9 8 7 6 5 4 3 2 1

BIG CHAPTER BOOKS is a trademark of Berenstain Enterprises, Inc.

Contents

Chapter 1
Operation Substitute

It was almost time for the school bell to ring when Brother Bear, Sister Bear, and Cousin Freddy reached the schoolyard one crisp fall morning. The schoolyard was packed with cubs. For many of them it would be a day like any other. But for the cubs in Teacher Bob's class, today was dif-

ferent. It was the first day of Teacher Bob's honeymoon at Great Grizzly Falls.

"Well," said Brother Bear as Barry and Lizzy Bruin came up to greet them. "Have you heard anything yet? Who's our sub?"

Brother and Freddy and Barry were all in Teacher Bob's class. They had been wondering about the substitute teacher all weekend.

"Her name is Ms. Barr," said Barry. "I just heard it from Too-Tall."

"Since when are you hanging around with Too-Tall?" asked Brother.

"Since I heard we're going to have a sub," said Barry. "Get it?" he added with a big grin.

Brother got it all right. It didn't surprise him that Too-Tall was already laying plans for the substitute. After all, it was almost as if you were *supposed* to have a little fun with a sub. But what did surprise Brother was that he was grinning a little himself.

"I hope you boys can control yourselves," said Lizzy Bruin. "We heard about those tricks you pulled the last time you had a sub."

"You mean, dropping our pencils all at once and crossing our legs at the same time?" said Barry. "That was Too-Tall's idea."

"No excuse," said Sister. "There's no

place in the classroom for that kind of behavior."

"Hey, you sound just like a teacher," said Barry, laughing.

"Well, maybe I'll be a teacher when I grow up," said Sister.

"Oh?" said Brother. "Will that be *before* or *after* you become a ballerina *and* an airplane pilot?"

"I'm not sure," said Sister. "I'll have to think about it."

"Don't worry, girls," said Barry. "We'll be

as nice as can be to our poor little substitute teacher. If we aren't, you can report us to Mr. Grizzmeyer." Barry looked off across the schoolyard. "Hey, what do you think Too-Tall wants?"

Too-Tall Grizzly was waving at the cubs. It looked as if he wanted them to come

over. Skuzz, Smirk, and Vinnie were with him.

"Probably some kind of trick," grumbled Freddy. "Like the time he pushed me backward over Skuzz."

"Hey, you guys!" yelled Too-Tall. "Get over here!"

"I think he just wants to talk to us," said Brother. "Let's go see."

All five cubs made their way through the crowd to Too-Tall.

"Not you two," snarled Too-Tall at Sister and Lizzy. "This is man talk. Get lost—both of you. Scram!"

Sister and Lizzy stuck out their tongues at Too-Tall. Then they skipped off to where some of their friends were jumping rope. "What's up, Too-Tall?" asked Brother. "Foot-stomps or Indian burns?"

Too-Tall had all kinds of mean tricks he'd pull on cubs. He'd stomp on your foot. Or he'd point to your jacket. Then, when you looked down, he'd zip his finger up and pop you on the nose. But Indian burns were the worst. He would grab your wrist with both his big hands and twist in opposite directions. It really hurt.

"Don't worry," said Too-Tall. "Nothin' like that today. I need your help."

"With what?" asked Barry.

"With our cute little sub, Ms. Barr."

"She's cute?" said Barry.

"Yeah. But more important, she's a pushover. At least that's what I hear."

"What'll it be this time?" asked Freddy. "Pencil-drops and leg-crosses again?"

"Sure, but that's only part of it," said Too-Tall. "We've got this sub for a whole week, guys. *A whole week!* Do you know what that means?"

"What?" asked Brother.

"It means we can do more than just bug her. We can BREAK her."

"What do you mean?" asked Barry.

"We can push her and push her until she can't take any more. The guys here are already betting on how long it'll take."

"Three days, tops," said Smirk.

"Nah, two," said Skuzz.

"You're both wrong," said Too-Tall. "I say

we'll break her in one day. By recess tomorrow morning, Ms. Barr won't be fit to teach another minute. Not after Operation Substitute!"

Brother Bear looked at Cousin Freddy. Cousin Freddy looked at Barry Bruin. Too-Tall really meant business this time! The nasty look in his eye was brighter than usual. But was it really a *nasty* look? Maybe it was just a *fun-loving* look. And what was

wrong with having a little fun with a sub?

"So what's the plan for this morning?" asked Brother.

"For you guys, nothin' yet," said Too-Tall. "Just sit tight until recess, then report to me. We're gonna be as nice as can be to Ms. Barr before recess. We'll make her think everything's cool. Then, when the bell rings for recess, we'll start in on her. Skuzz, you've got your orders."

"Right, boss."

Just then the bell rang. Too-Tall and his gang were usually the last ones into the building. And they were always a few minutes late for class. But today they were so eager to get to class that they pushed ahead of everyone else.

After lining up to go inside, Brother, Freddy, and Barry looked back and saw Sister and Lizzy frowning at them.

"Who are we gonna listen to?" Barry said to Brother. "Too-Tall or a couple of little sisters?"

"There's no harm in having a little fun with a sub, is there?" said Brother.

"Right on," said Barry.

Besides, thought Brother, it felt good to be part of the gang for a change. It felt more grown-up.

Chapter 2
Ms. Barr and the Airplane

Ms. Barr started the class in the way all subs did. First she wrote her name on the board. Then she asked the cubs to raise their hands when she called the roll. They all did, except for Too-Tall and the gang. They had to show off by yelling "Present!" "Here!" and "Yo!"

Then Ms. Barr told the class a little about herself. She told them that she had just moved from Bruinville, where she had often been a substitute. But this was her first time teaching at Bear Country School. She also said that she saw one face she already knew. That was the face of Bertha Broom, who

had also just moved from Bruinville.

Just as Too-Tall had promised, no pranks were pulled on Ms. Barr all through roll call, all through her talk about herself, or all through the earth-science lesson that followed.

When the bell rang for morning recess, the cubs began to file out of the room. As Ms. Barr bent down over her desk to close her earth-science book, Too-Tall nodded to Skuzz. Skuzz pulled out a paper airplane from behind his back and let it fly at Ms. Barr. The airplane rose toward the ceiling and then came down and poked its pointy nose under Ms. Barr's headband. She was a funny sight with a paper airplane sticking out of her head.

Too-Tall and the gang began snickering. Brother, Freddy, and Barry started snickering too. Then they made their way to the door. As they looked back, they saw Ms. Barr unfolding the paper airplane and read-

ing the message printed on it. She was trying to look calm. But the cubs could tell
that she wasn't.

Out in the schoolyard, Brother, Freddy,
and Barry reported to Too-Tall. "Nice shot,
Skuzz," Too-Tall was saying. "What did you
write on it?"

"Nothin' fancy," said Skuzz. "Just 'Wel-
come to the Bear Country School.' A
warmup for the better stuff to come."

"Perfect," said Too-Tall. "We'll start slow this morning. Then we'll turn up the heat in the afternoon. Finally, we'll pull out all the stops tomorrow morning. By morning recess, Ms. Barr will be so messed up she won't even remember her own name."

"What's the plan for now until lunch-time?" asked Barry.

"Simple," said Too-Tall. "First we do the leg-cross. Then we do the pencil-drop. One cough from me means count to three and

cross your leg. Start with left over right and change on each cough. Two coughs from me means count to ten and drop your pencil on the floor. Then, at the lunch bell, another airplane from the unfriendly skies of Skuzz Airways. Since your aim was so good the first time, Skuzz, I'm letting you do the honors again."

"Thanks, boss," said Skuzz. He grinned proudly.

Too-Tall pointed to Brother, Freddy, and Barry. "You three tell the other guys about the leg-crossing and pencil-dropping. Forget about the girls. They always take the teacher's side anyway. Besides, breakin' subs is MAN'S work. Come on, what're ya waitin' for, guys? Get movin'!"

Brother had a sudden urge to say "Okay, boss," but caught himself. After all, he wasn't really a member of the gang. But it felt good for a change to be a part of a real group with a real plan. And it felt good to have something more important to do at recess than play ball.

Brother had just finished telling the plan to some of the guys when Sister and Lizzy came over. "Well, well," said Sister, "if it isn't the Great Sub-Breaker himself. What's going on with Ms. Barr?"

"Nothing much," said Brother. "We didn't do anything all morning. Skuzz just tossed one little paper airplane."

"Which hit Ms. Barr right on the head and got a big laugh," added Lizzy. "My big-mouth brother told me."

"It didn't hurt her," said Brother.

"So what's next on the list of tortures?" asked Sister.

"A little leg-cross, a little pencil-drop.

Just silly stuff," said Brother.

"That's not what Barry says," said Lizzy. "He says there's something called Operation Substitute. He says you're gonna push Ms. Barr until she breaks. That doesn't sound like 'just silly stuff' to me."

"Oh, come off it," said Brother, groaning. "You're making too much out of this. We're just having a little fun."

"Okay, that's *your* story," said Sister. "See you at lunch. Maybe."

Boy, thought Brother as Sister and Lizzy wandered off. Little sisters can be such a pain!

SEE YOU AT LUNCH-MAYBE!

Chapter 3
Turning Up the Heat

When the cubs returned to class after morning recess, Ms. Barr looked very calm again. It seemed almost as if Skuzz's paper airplane had never been thrown. Brother leaned over to Freddy and whispered, "Wow, I thought she'd still be mad."

Then Too-Tall leaned forward from behind and said, "Yeah, it's perfect. She's trying hard to be patient with us. We've got her right where we want her, guys."

Brother had two different feelings just then. First, he felt a little sorry for Ms. Barr. She seemed to be such a nice teacher and was trying so hard to be patient. But all the boys in the class were plotting against her. On the other hand, Brother felt good being part of Too-Tall's plan and being called "one of the guys" by Too-Tall.

Brother knew that a lot of the things that Too-Tall and the gang did were wrong. But at the same time, he couldn't help sort of looking up to Too-Tall. And it wasn't just because of Too-Tall's height! Too-Tall Griz-

zly was a natural leader. And he was older than Brother.

Sometimes, when Brother stood up to Too-Tall, Too-Tall seemed to admire him. But Too-Tall had never really seemed to *like* Brother. Now that Brother was part of Operation Substitute, Too-Tall was treating him like a friend. That made Brother feel good.

"Quiet now, cubs. It's time for math," said Ms. Barr in a friendly voice. She walked to the blackboard and started doing a long-division problem.

When she was about halfway done, Too-Tall let out a loud cough. Ms. Barr stopped writing and turned to look in Too-Tall's direction. An instant later, all the boys crossed their legs at once, left over right. There were a few giggles from the girls. Ms. Barr looked confused. She turned back to the blackboard and started writing again.

A moment later, Too-Tall coughed again. Ms. Barr looked over her shoulder in time to see all the boys cross their legs, right over left. Still, she turned back to the blackboard without saying anything.

Too-Tall leaned toward Brother and whispered, "Great. She thinks we'll stop if she ignores us. Keep up the good work. COUGH!"

One, two, three, left leg over right.

Ms. Barr didn't even turn around this time. Too-Tall let her finish the problem on the board, then...

COUGH! COUGH!

Now Ms. Barr lost her patience. She whirled around and stared angrily at the boys' legs. She waited for them to move. But nothing happened! What are they up to this time? she wondered.

...seven, eight, nine, ten. CLICK!

CLANK! CLATTER! All the boys dropped their pencils on the floor at once. Pencils rattled and rolled into every nook and cranny of the classroom. Cubs got down on

their hands and knees and crawled around the floor looking for them. Freddy's had rolled all the way to the front of the room. And it had come to rest right in between Ms. Barr's feet. Freddy hurried up to snatch the pencil. He gave Ms. Barr a great big silly grin and said, "Sorry...heh heh." Then he crept back to his seat. The whole class broke into laughter.

Ms. Barr stood with arms folded. She stared at the class. She knew that every

class has its troublemakers. And it was clear that the troublemakers in this class were Too-Tall and his gang.

Ms. Barr looked straight at Too-Tall. "All right," she said. "We've all had a little fun, and no real harm has been done. But we have work to do. My job is to teach. And your job is to learn. From here on I want some cooperation. So here's the deal. All of you who agree to cooperate, raise your hands."

All the girls raised their hands. Most of the boys followed Too-Tall. His hand was raised the highest of all. And he was grinning.

"All right now. That's a promise," said Ms. Barr. "Now let's get back to work."

But Ms. Barr had forgotten about the unfriendly skies of Skuzz Airways. The lunch bell rang. *Zoom!* Paper Airplane Two circled round and round Ms. Barr and did a loop-the-loop into her ear. It was a funny sight. But this time there wasn't any snick-

ering. Instead, there was a lot of hands-over-the-mouth choking laughter. And it came from the boys *and* the girls.

But there was one girl who didn't laugh. Bertha Broom. Bertha usually didn't have much to say. Except, that is, on the football field, where actions spoke louder than words. There she knocked over boy players like tenpins. Bertha spoke only when she had something really important to say. And when she spoke, cubs listened.

Bertha, who was as big as Too-Tall, stood up and looked out over the class. "There are certain things you don't know," she said in a quiet voice. "But I'll tell you something. Some of you are headed for trouble. BIG trouble."

"That will be enough, Bertha," said Ms. Barr.

"But Ms. Barr…"

"I said, 'that will be enough,' " said Ms. Barr again.

What was Bertha talking about? wondered the cubs. What *kind* of big trouble?

Chapter 4
More Plans

In the lunchroom, Brother, Freddy, and Barry usually sat with Sister and Lizzy. But today they sat with Too-Tall and the gang.

The gang was having a lot of fun talking about what had happened so far. When Too-Tall got to the part about the airplane in Ms. Barr's ear, everyone roared with laughter.

"That was an even better shot than the first one, Skuzz," said Too-Tall. "By the way, what did you write on it this time?"

"I wrote: 'So much for cooperation. Stay tuned…'!"

Everyone burst out laughing again.

Brother Bear laughed along with the others. But he was also feeling sorry for Ms. Barr. Neither of the paper airplanes had hurt her. But what if one of them had hit her in the eye? Paper airplanes could be dangerous. He hoped that maybe Too-Tall would forget about them. Then he tried to think of tricks that weren't dangerous.

"Hey!" Too-Tall yelled in Brother's ear. He snapped his fingers in Brother's face.

"Er—huh?" said Brother.

"Are you part of Operation Substitute or not?" said Too-Tall. "We're having a war council here, and you're a million miles away! I'm asking for ideas about stuff we can pull on the sub. You got any?"

"A frog," said Brother.

"A frog?" said Too-Tall.

"Yeah. A giant bullfrog," said Brother. "We'll put it on the desk when she's not looking. It could be really funny—a big old bullfrog plopping around the room. I can just hear all the girls screaming." Then Brother added, under his breath, "And it won't hurt anybody."

Too-Tall scratched his chin and thought.

"Bullfrog," he said. "I like it. Let's do it."

"I don't know," said Freddy. "That frog could get us all reported to Mr. Grizzmeyer."

"Nah," said Too-Tall. "Ms. Barr won't go to Grizzmeyer. I know her type. She wants to take care of it herself. Reporting us to Grizzmeyer would be a defeat."

"Then let's go for it!" cried Barry Bruin.

"That's the spirit," said Too-Tall. "But the frog isn't enough. We need more."

Freddy thought. He didn't want to be outdone by Brother. "How about frog calls?" he said. "When Brother puts the frog on Ms. Barr's desk, we could all do frog calls."

Too-Tall turned proudly to his gang. "What did I tell ya, fellas? The boy's a genius." Freddy beamed.

The war council moved from the lunch-

room to the schoolyard for recess. Then Too-Tall ordered Brother and Freddy to sneak off to Frog Pond. "Who's got a bag for Brother?" he asked the gang. No one answered. "What's that hangin' out of your back pocket, Skuzz?"

Skuzz stuffed the burlap bag deep into his pocket. "But boss!" he cried. "I was gonna fill it with rocks for breakin' windows at Paddy McBear's warehouse down by the train station!"

"Hand it over," said Too-Tall. "First things

first. We need that bullfrog right away."

"Who would have thought I could turn those two straight arrows into good solid criminals?" said Too-Tall proudly as soon as Brother and Freddy had gone.

"Not me, boss," said Skuzz.

"You're great, boss," said Smirk.

"Full of surprises, boss," added Vinnie.

"It's kind of nice to get some new blood and fresh ideas into the gang," said Too-Tall. He turned to Barry Bruin. "These three stooges get boring after a while. Now, what about you, Barry? You haven't come up with an idea yet. The frog and the frog calls are fine. But we need more. We need something more...*disgusting*."

Barry thought hard. He didn't want to be shown up by Brother and Freddy. Finally, he leaned over and whispered something in

Too-Tall's ear. Too-Tall nodded. "Good," he said. "I like it."

"Tell us, boss," said Skuzz.

Too-Tall turned to the gang. "Class, what's made of paper and is small, round, and very wet?" he asked.

Smirk raised his hand. "Oh, I know, teacher!"

"Yes, Smirk?"

"A SPITBALL!"

"Very good, Smirk," said Too-Tall. "Not only do you get a star next to your name. You also get to throw the first spitball!"

I LIKE IT.

Meanwhile, Brother and Freddy were walking down the narrow path through the woods toward Frog Pond. Freddy looked worried. Brother asked him what was wrong.

"It's Operation Substitute," said Freddy.

"I'm afraid it's going to get out of hand. Especially with Too-Tall calling the shots."

"I've been thinking the same thing," said Brother. "But I don't see how we can stop it unless we rat on Too-Tall." He thought for a moment. "Maybe the frog prank will be enough to get Too-Tall to end Operation Substitute," he said. "If it isn't, we can think up some less harmful stuff for him."

"Let's hope the frog *is* enough," said Freddy.

Frog Pond was across the railroad tracks

that ran through the woods between Beartown and Bruinville. The cubs made sure no train was coming and crossed the tracks. They crept silently up to Frog Pond and hid behind some tall cattails. Before long they spotted a giant bullfrog sunning himself on a log at the water's edge. Brother sneaked up, snatched the frog, and stuffed

him into his burlap bag. He and Freddy hurried back to school.

At the schoolyard, Sister Bear and Lizzy Bruin saw Brother and Freddy slip through a hole in the fence and run over to the Too-Tall gang. The girls strolled up to the gang. "What are you guys planning for the afternoon?" asked Lizzy. "An atom bomb?"

"Hey, who are these two little squirts?" said Too-Tall. "The Substitute Teacher Police?"

"We heard all about the paper airplane in Ms. Barr's ear," said Sister. "What if it had hit her in the eye?"

The gang laughed. Brother swallowed hard and laughed along with the others. He knew Sister was right. But he didn't want the gang to know he thought so.

"What's in the bag, Brother?" asked Sister. "A hand grenade?"

"Hey, pipsqueak," snarled Too-Tall. "What's in the bag ain't none of your business. Ain't that right, Brother?"

Brother turned on his sister. "Yeah!" he barked. "That's right! Now get lost, girls. Go play hopscotch or something. We've got serious business to take care of."

"Okay, have it your way," said Sister.

As the girls walked away, Lizzy said to Sister, "I don't like this one bit, Sister Bear."

"Me neither," said Sister. "This morning it was 'just silly stuff.' Now it's 'serious business!' "

Chapter 5
A Froggy Afternoon

During lunch Ms. Barr studied Teacher Bob's roll book. It was pretty clear that most members of the class were good, well-behaved cubs. And it was just as clear that Too-Tall and his gang were big behavior problems.

Ms. Barr began making a plan. She figured that if she could get the good cubs interested in a subject, the bad apples—Too-Tall and his gang—might settle back down to the bottom of the barrel.

History was the first lesson after lunch. History was Ms. Barr's favorite subject. It had been her major in college. She had even shot a terrific video of Great Grizzly

National Park, Bear Country's most historic area.

After lunch Ms. Barr told the class that she had a real treat for them. The next day she would show them her video.

Ms. Barr knew that the cubs would be looking forward to the video all day. She hoped this would help them behave themselves. She made the video sound really interesting. She said it showed the log cabins at Grizzly Forge. That was where long, long ago, Bear Country's soldiers spent a very hard winter. Then she said they would see Mount Grizzmore, the famous

mountain that had Bear Country's heroes carved in its side. And of course the cubs would see Great Grizzly Falls, the very falls that ran Bear Country's first mill.

"And speaking of Great Grizzly Falls," said Ms. Barr, "that's just where Teacher Bob is on his honeymoon. Which reminds me—part of the job of a substitute teacher is to write a report. And that report will be on Teacher Bob's desk the moment he returns."

It was a pretty good speech. And it should have worked. It had a carrot: the really terrific video of Great Grizzly National Park. It had a stick: the report Teacher Bob would find on his desk when he returned.

There were just two problems: Too-Tall didn't like carrots and he wasn't afraid of sticks.

Ms. Barr began the history lesson. First she talked about the founding of Bear Country by Jedidiah Bruin. But just as she started to write "Jedidiah Bruin" on the blackboard—SPLAT—a big juicy spitball hit the blackboard just above her head. She decided to keep going.

"As Teacher Bob probably told you," Ms. Barr went on, "Jedidiah Bruin not only founded Bear Country, but he built its first mill.... And that mill was powered by what, class?"

"Great Grizzly Falls," said Betsy Bruin. Betsy was very tuned in. That was because Jedidiah Bruin was her great-great-great-grandfather.

"Very good," said Ms. Barr. She began to write "J. Bruin—built first mill" on the blackboard.

SPLAT!

The second spitball was much bigger than the first. It was so big it didn't stick to the blackboard. It slid down the blackboard, leaving a wet trail like a big gray slug.

Ms. Barr turned and faced the class. "All

right," she said. "Since your country's history doesn't interest you, let's shift to English. We'll begin with parts of speech. I'll write down some sentences on the board using parts of speech that you give me."

SPLAT! SPLAT! SPLAT!

Three more spitballs whizzed past Ms. Barr's head and stuck to the blackboard.

Brother Bear squirmed in his seat. This was not only *not* fun. It was awful. Operation Substitute was turning into Operation Big Wet Sloppy Spitball. Soon one of those big, wet, sloppy spitballs would hit poor Ms. Barr.

Brother had to do something. But what could he do? He was thinking very hard

when he happened to look over at Skuzz. Skuzz's cheek was bulging like a balloon. He was tearing bits of paper from his notebook and stuffing them into his mouth. There was no question about what Skuzz was doing. He was making a super-gigantic spit-ball—a *Skuzz*ball.

Brother *had* to do something! Suddenly he remembered the frog! He had almost forgotten about it. While Ms. Barr wrote the word "The" on the board, Brother took the big bullfrog out of its bag and put it on Ms. Barr's desk. *That* got everybody's attention. Everybody, that is, except Ms. Barr. She was still facing the blackboard.

"All right, then," said Ms. Barr. "Let's start our sentence. Someone give me a noun."

"Frog!" shouted Queenie, choking down a giggle.

"Ribbit! Ribbit!" shouted Barry. Soon the rest of the class was "ribbiting" along with him.

"All right," said Ms. Barr. "Give me an action word."

"Jumps!" someone shouted. Not that the frog was jumping. It was just sitting there half asleep.

In the meantime, Skuzz's mind was stuck on spitballs. He had taken the great ugly thing out of his mouth and was getting ready to launch it. In a split second, the Mother of All Spitballs would be whizzing toward the back of Ms. Barr's head at warp speed. There was no time to think. Four-three-two-one—LAUNCH! Brother leaped up to block the awful saliva bomb with his backpack!

But Brother heard no splat. Had he figured the path of the giant Skuzzball wrong? No. What Brother figured wrong was Skuzz. Skuzz hadn't aimed at the back of Ms. Barr's head at all. He had aimed at the frog. He wanted to make it jump. And jump it did. It jumped at the same moment

that Ms. Barr finally lost her temper and whirled around to face the class.

The frog landed smack on her shoulder. She shrieked as it slid under her collar and down her back. She reached for it. But it had slid so far down that it was trapped at her beltline. Ms. Barr did a wild, twisting dance. She screamed and shrieked as the slippery bullfrog wriggled around inside her blouse.

When the frog made its leap, the whole class had exploded with laughter. But now the laughter died down very quickly. Only Too-Tall and his gang tried to keep the "fun" going by clapping their hands to the beat of Ms. Barr's crazy dance. "Hey!" yelled Too-Tall. "A new dance! The frog hop!"

"Too-Tall," said Bertha Broom. "Why don't you shut up?" Then she, Babs, and Queenie helped Ms. Barr out into the hall

toward the Girls' Room.

At that moment, Brother Bear felt like the worst, lowest, rottenest cub on earth. The whole horrible history of Operation Substitute flashed before him: joining up with Too-Tall; almost becoming a *member* of the gang; the stupid leg-crossings; the creepy pencil-dropping; the totally disgusting spitballs; and finally, his own idea— THE FROG. Operation Substitute was wrong. It was wrong, wrong, wrong. And now Brother felt awful, awful, awful.

But there was one good thing about the frog—one very good thing. Surely this would be the end of Operation Substitute. Too-Tall's goal was to "break" Ms. Barr. And break her they did.

Brother was in a gloomy world of his own when he sensed that Ms. Barr had come back into the room. She was angry. Her eyes flashed. The bullfrog sat in her hands. "Class," she said, "I'm going to ask this question only once. And I want an answer

before I count to ten. WHOSE FROG IS THIS? One…two…"

"It's mine!" cried Brother, jumping up.

"And I helped!" said Freddy.

Ms. Barr was surprised. She knew from Teacher Bob's roll book that Brother and Freddy were not big troublemakers. In fact, she was sure that Too-Tall and his gang were behind the frog prank and all the rest of the troubles. She decided to wait and see if she could catch Too-Tall the next time he tried something.

"Sit down, you two," Ms. Barr said to Brother and Freddy. "I haven't decided what I'm going to do about you. But please take your froggy friend off my hands." Brother blushed deep red as he took back the frog and stuffed it into its bag.

Later that afternoon, Brother and Freddy headed home from school together. Sister and Lizzy tagged along. The news of Ms. Barr and the frog had spread quickly through the school. So of course Sister and Lizzy knew all about it.

Hands in his pockets, Brother stared at the ground as he walked. He didn't say a word all the way home. Finally he spoke. "Are you going to tell?" he asked.

"Tell what?" said Sister.

"You know what I mean," Brother said. "Tell Mama and Papa."

"I'm no squealer," said Sister.

Brother turned to Lizzy. "How about you?"

"I haven't decided," said Lizzy. "My

brother can be an awful pain. I'll have to think about it."

Brother sighed and sank back into his worried thoughts. He was so deep in thought that he didn't hear Freddy talking to him.

"Hey!" yelled Freddy. "Where are you?"

"Huh?" said Brother. "Oh, on the planet Pluto. Or on one of the outer rings of Saturn. As far away as I can get from this awful Operation Substitute."

"I asked you if you saw Bertha and Ms. Barr talking after class," Freddy said.

"No," said Brother. "What were they talking about?"

"Bertha was trying to get Ms. Barr to let her out of a promise of some sort," said Freddy. "Something she's not supposed to tell the rest of the class. I think it's some kind of secret about Ms. Barr."

"Hmm, a secret about Ms. Barr." Brother shook his head. "I've got more important things to worry about, Freddy. And so should you. What are you going to tell your parents about the frog prank?"

"Frog prank?" said Freddy, raising his eyebrows. "What frog prank?"

Brother got it. Freddy wasn't going to tell his parents *anything* about the frog prank. That might be okay for Freddy. But Brother had always been pretty honest with his parents. If he told them, they might not be too hard on him. But if they heard about it from someone else, there was no telling what his punishment might be. Grounded for life sounded about right. Brother sighed another big sigh.

"Will you please stop that sighing?" said Sister. "It's getting on my nerves."

Chapter 6
New News Is Bad News

That evening at the Bear family's tree house, Brother Bear was very quiet all through dinner. When Papa asked him how things had gone at school, he just mumbled, "Okay." He didn't even look up. It was pretty clear to Mama that Brother had something on his mind.

Later the cubs sat on the sofa in the living room watching the news on TV. They weren't really paying attention, though. Both were thinking hard, especially Brother. To tell or not to tell? That was the question.

Mama came quietly into the living room and switched off the TV. Sister knew why right away. Mama knew that something was troubling Brother. Now she was going to ask him about it. And no matter how embarrassed Brother was, he was going to tell her the whole story. That was what always happened.

"Well, I guess it's time to start my homework," said Sister. She headed upstairs.

Brother was so upset that he hadn't even noticed that the TV was off or that Sister had left.

"Brother?" said Mama gently.

Brother looked up in a daze. "Huh? What?"

"I know something is bothering you," said Mama. "Seems like something pretty serious. Would you like to tell me about it?"

Brother sighed. It was all so embarrassing. He couldn't stand the thought of his parents knowing. On the other hand, keeping it a secret from them was wearing him out. Before he knew it, he was telling Mama the whole story of Operation Substitute and the frog prank.

"Well," said Mama when Brother had finished. "That's quite a story. It sounds as though you've been trying too hard to make the wrong people like you."

Brother nodded. "Not anymore, though," he said. "I quit Operation Substitute this afternoon. So did Cousin Freddy. I think it's over anyway. Not even Too-Tall would want to push Ms. Barr any further."

"Your papa is going to have to hear all about this, you know." Mama called to Papa, who came in from the kitchen spooning the last fresh raspberries from a dessert bowl. Mama told him the whole story. As she spoke, Papa's frown got deeper and deeper. By the time Mama had finished, Papa looked ready to explode. And explode he did.

"That's a disgrace!" he yelled. "I've never heard of worse behavior in school! Brother must be punished. He's grounded for a week! A month! A year!"

"For life," said Brother, under his breath.

Mama raised a hand. "Now just a minute, Papa," she said. "It seems to me that Ms. Barr must have had a good reason for not punishing Brother herself. I think it probably was because she knows that Brother's behavior record is one of the best in Bear Country School. I think she knew that Too-Tall was behind all this nonsense. And don't forget that Brother confessed right away. I think we can go along with Ms. Barr and not punish Brother this time."

Papa was still frowning. "Well, maybe…"

"And as for your never hearing of worse behavior in school, Papa—I'm not so sure of that."

"What's that supposed to mean?" asked Papa.

"I remember a young cub—not a bad cub, really—at Bear Country School, years ago, who did something just as bad to Miss Grizzle when she was a substitute teacher."

"What did he do?" asked Papa.

"He put a salamander in her lunch bag," said Mama. She stared straight at Papa. "The salamander crawled right into her egg-

salad sandwich. And the young cub wasn't brave enough to confess right away. Remember?"

Papa gave a sheepish grin. "Oh, yeah," he said. "I remember. Heh heh. Long time ago. We'll go easy on you this time, Brother. But don't ever do anything like that again."

"Don't worry, I won't," said Brother.

Just then the phone rang. Papa answered it. "Oh, hi, Lizzy," he said. "Just a minute." He called upstairs. "Sister Bear! Phone call!"

Brother passed Sister on the stairs as he headed up to start his homework. A few minutes later, Sister came bursting into his room. "Hey!" he said. "Ever hear of knocking?"

"But this is important!" said Sister. "Lizzy heard from Barry that Too-Tall is not calling off Operation Substitute. In fact, tomorrow

71

morning Too-Tall and the gang are planning to turn Ms. Barr's Great Grizzly National Park video into a total disaster."

Brother was shocked. "That's awful!" he said.

"And Barry's such a blabbermouth," said Sister, "that he told Lizzy the whole plan!"

"Well, for Pete's sake, let's hear it!" said Brother.

TOO-TALL IS NOT CALLING OFF OPERATION SUBSTITUTE!

DO NOT DISTURB

"Okay," said Sister. "Too-Tall and the gang are going to sneak into school early tomorrow morning. They're going to remove a ceiling tile right above where Ms. Barr will most likely stand for the video. Then they're going to get into the crawl-space and rig up a bucket of water with a stick for a prop and a string. When the video gets to the part about Great Grizzly Falls, Too-Tall will yank the string. That will pull the prop, which will send a bucketful of cold water down on Ms. Barr. He says he wants to make her CRY in front of the class. That's what he means by 'breaking' her!"

Brother could only shake his head in disbelief. "Make her cry in class," he said. "That's really sick. It would be the worst prank Too-Tall ever pulled."

"WOULD be?" said Sister. "Don't you think he'll go through with it?"

"I think he'll try to," said Brother. "But I don't think he'll succeed."

"Why not?"

"Because I'm going to stop him," said Brother. "I'll go to school early tomorrow morning and tell Ms. Barr the whole story."

"You mean you're gonna squeal?" said Sister.

"What choice do I have?" asked Brother.

"But Too-Tall and the gang will hate you forever," said Sister. "And what about Barry? He's your friend."

Brother shook his head again. "It can't be helped."

Make Ms. Barr cry, thought Brother. It was the meanest, nastiest plan that the big bully had ever come up with. Brother would be proud to put an end to it.

Chapter 7
Video Folly

The next morning, Brother was all ready to go to school when Papa stopped him. "Leaving kind of early, aren't you, son?" asked Papa.

"I've got something to take care of before school starts," said Brother.

"I'll say you do," said Papa. "The bullfrog. That poor guy shouldn't have to spend another night stuck in that little fishbowl on the kitchen counter."

"I forgot," said Brother. "I'll put him in our stream."

"Oh, no," said Papa. "You'll take him back to the pond where you got him. His family and friends are all there."

No problem, thought Brother. There was still time to pick up Freddy, cut over to Frog Pond on the way to school, and get to class in time to put a stop to Too-Tall's nasty plan.

Brother put the bullfrog in a lunch bag and walked to Cousin Freddy's. From there the cubs cut through the woods and across the railroad tracks to Frog Pond. Brother found the same fallen log that the frog had been sitting on before. He slid the sleeping frog out of the bag and onto the log. The moment its hind legs touched the log, the bullfrog sprang into the pond.

"Look at him go!" said Freddy.

"I'll bet he's glad to be home again," said

Brother. He looked at his wristwatch. "Come on," he said. "We still have time to get to class if we walk fast."

"Wait a minute," said Freddy. He was listening to something in the distance. "Do you hear what I hear?"

Brother listened. He heard it. A whistle. A TRAIN whistle. "Uh-oh!" he said. "We'd better hurry!"

The cubs ran toward the railroad tracks. But they were too late. The train was already near. Helplessly, they stood and watched it go by. It was a long, slow-moving freight train.

"…nine…ten…," said Freddy.

"What are you doing?" asked Brother.

"Counting the cars," said Freddy. "…thirteen…fourteen…"

"We're gonna be late for class!" groaned Brother. "And Ms. Barr is supposed to show the video first thing in the morning!"

"…twenty…twenty-one…," said Freddy.

"What will we do?" cried Brother.

"…twenty-four…twenty-five…," counted Freddy.

Brother fell silent. It was many minutes before the red caboose finally came into view and rattled past them.

"A hundred and sixteen!" said Freddy. "Wow!"

"Sometimes you kill me," said Brother. "Come on! Run!"

The cubs dashed across the railroad tracks and ran down the path toward school.

Meanwhile, Ms. Barr was nearly ready to show her home video of Great Grizzly National Park. If she had looked up, she might have noticed that a ceiling tile was missing just to the left of the TV. That was where Teacher Bob always stood to show videos and slides.

Too-Tall Grizzly sat quietly in his seat. He prayed that no one would notice the string that ran from his hand to the spot on the ceiling where the tile was missing.

Vinnie leaned in from behind Too-Tall. "Hey, boss," he whispered, "where are those two wimpy traitors?"

"You mean, Brother Bear and his nerdy cousin?" said Too-Tall. "Must be sick. Or late for school."

"If they're just late," said Vinnie, "they could still mess us up. Walt Grizzwald told me he heard our whole plan from that blabbermouth Barry Bruin. Who knows who else he blabbed to?"

"Not to worry," said Too-Tall. "Even if they get here before Great Grizzly Falls comes up on the video, they can't do nothin'."

"Why not, boss?" asked Vinnie.

"Because I locked the door."

"Good thinkin', boss."

Ms. Barr nodded to Bertha Broom to

start the VCR. Then she turned off the lights. Too-Tall gave a sigh of relief. Brother Bear and Freddy hadn't shown up. And no one had noticed the string. Too-Tall's grand water prank was all set to go.

Ms. Barr stood next to the TV and began describing what was on the screen. "These crude log cabins at Grizzly Forge," she said, "are copies of the ones in which a ragged bear army spent a hard winter during the War of Independence. No electricity and no hot water, cubs. Bears were tougher in those days."

Next came a beautiful shot of Mount Grizzmore against a brilliant blue sky. The faces of Jedidiah Bruin and other founders of Bear Country stared back at the cubs. "It took our great sculptor, Abner Brunoski, twenty years to chisel those faces out of Mount Grizzmore," said Ms. Barr.

Suddenly Too-Tall gasped. Ms. Barr wasn't standing to the left of the screen under the bucket of water. She was standing to the *right* of the screen! A shot of Great Grizzly Falls might be next in the video! Too-Tall looked around quickly. Skuzz was sitting at the far right of the room. That gave Too-Tall an idea. He threw an eraser at Skuzz to get his attention. Then he pointed back and forth between Ms. Barr and the hole in the ceiling. Skuzz caught on.

"Stop the movie!" cried Skuzz. Bertha

Broom hit the pause button. The video froze on a view of Grizzly Lake.

"What's wrong?" asked Ms. Barr.

"You're blockin' my view, Ms. Barr," said Skuzz. "Would you mind moving to the other side of the TV?"

"Not at all," said Ms. Barr. She was pleased that Skuzz had asked so politely. She crossed to the other side. "There, how's that?" she asked.

"Fine," said Skuzz.

Ms. Barr looked over at Smirk, who was sitting at the far left of the room. "What about you, Smirk?" she asked. "Can you see?"

"Oh, yes, Ms. Barr," said Smirk sweetly. Then he sneaked a look at the hole in the ceiling. "That's perfect," he said. "Don't move an inch."

Bertha started the video again. Ms. Barr

finished discussing the history of Grizzly Lake. Next, a majestic view of vast Great Grizzly Falls—with its tons of rushing water—lit up the screen.

At that very moment, Brother and Freddy finally arrived. They began pounding on the classroom door. But they were too late.

For at the same moment, Too-Tall pulled the string, which made the bucket turn over. Ice-cold water came pouring down on Ms. Barr's head.

The gang and some of the other boys laughed as Ms. Barr shrieked and fell backward in the spreading puddle of water. They laughed even louder as she slipped and slid around on the floor, trying to get up.

Soon someone turned on the lights and let Brother and Freddy in.

Had Too-Tall made Ms. Barr cry? Since her face was already soaked, no one could tell. But it certainly looked as if the gang had finally broken her spirit.

Queenie McBear and Babs Bruno rushed to Ms. Barr's aid. Brother and Freddy followed. All together they helped the teacher to her feet. Ms. Barr hurried out of the room. She left behind a sloppy, wet trail.

Chapter 8
A Startling Discovery

After Ms. Barr left the classroom, the cubs stood speechless. Most of them couldn't believe that Too-Tall had played such a nasty, embarrassing trick on the teacher. But nobody seemed to know what to do next.

Except Bertha Broom. She walked to the front of the classroom and barked, "In your seats!" Everyone took their seats. "There's something else on this tape," she said. "Something you all ought to see. Especially YOU, Too-Tall."

"Oh, boy, another movie!" shouted Too-Tall to his gang. "Hope it's as funny as the last one!"

Bertha marched back to the VCR. She fast-forwarded the tape to the end of the Great Grizzly National Park section. There on the screen was someone dressed in full karate uniform. And that someone was putting on a demonstration of karate moves and kicks.

"Cool," said Too-Tall. "And I'll bet Ms. Barr wasn't even going to show us this part."

"Shut up and watch, Too-Tall," said Bertha.

The cubs stared. They were fascinated by the rapid-fire moves of the karate expert. The demonstrator cut a wooden plank in half with one blow.

"Wow!" said Skuzz. "That board never had a chance."

The demonstrator smashed a pile of bricks to dust.

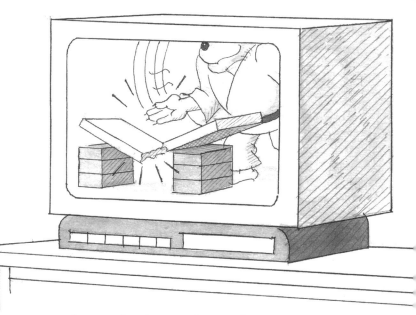

"Holy smokes!" cried Smirk.

The demonstrator tossed, threw, and slammed to the mat a series of big, burly fellows.

"Ouch," said Too-Tall. "I sure hope I never meet *her* in a dark alley." Wait a minute, thought Too-Tall. HER? He leaned forward for a closer look. Just as he did so, the home-video camera zoomed in for a closeup of the demonstrator's face. It was indeed a "she." And not just any old "she."

"Holy cow!" cried Too-Tall. "It's MS. BARR!"

The class let out one big gasp. Bertha switched off the VCR and turned on the lights. No one made a sound as she walked slowly to the front of the classroom.

"You're exactly right, Too-Tall," said Bertha softly. "That was Ms. Barr giving a demonstration at Bruinville School. She was celebrating her new black belt in karate."

"Wow!" said Barry Bruin. "Ms. Barr is a BLACK BELT!"

HOLY COW! IT'S MS. BARR!

"Well, Too-Tall, what do you think?" asked Bertha with a big smile.

Too-Tall sank down in his chair. He felt as if his bones were all turning to jelly. "What do I think?" he whined. "I...er...think you should have told me about it before I dropped a bucket of water on Ms. Barr's head." He was angry. "Why didn't you SAY something, Bertha?"

"Ms. Barr made me promise not to," said Bertha. "She was afraid it would scare all of you." Bertha looked straight at Too-Tall. "Well, are you SCARED?"

Too-Tall just hid his face in his hands and cried, "What am I gonna do?"

Just then the cubs heard a familiar voice. "CLASS!" They sat up straight in their chairs and didn't make a sound.

The school vice principal, "Bullhorn"

Grizzmeyer, stood in the open doorway. He marched to the front of the class. Then he ran his eyes along each row of cubs. "You're all suspended for the rest of the day," he growled. "The school secretary is busy calling your parents on the phone right now. Tomorrow you'll have a new substitute. Guess who?" He grinned.

The cubs gulped and rolled their eyes. Mr. Grizzmeyer in charge of class? What could be worse?

"I suggest you all get a good night's sleep," continued Mr. Grizzmeyer, "because I've got plans for you. NOW GET OUT OF HERE!"

No one stayed around to ask Mr. Grizzmeyer what his plans for them were. In an instant, the cubs were all crowded around the door, trying to get out. And the first one there was Too-Tall Grizzly.

Chapter 9
A Dazzling Demo

At the start of class the next morning, Mr. Grizzmeyer told the cubs to follow him to the gymnasium.

"Gymnasium?" said Cousin Freddy as they filed down the hall. "We never have gym class first thing in the morning."

"Something tells me it isn't gym class," said Brother Bear.

And Brother was right. When the cubs reached the gym, Mr. Grizzmeyer had them sit on the floor in front of some large mats. On the mats were several pieces of equipment. These included pieces for board-cracking and brick-smashing. Soon all the other classes began filing into the gym with their teachers.

"And now," said Mr. Grizzmeyer when everyone was seated, "I introduce our demonstrator, Ms. Black Belt Barr!"

Ms. Barr came running from the girls' locker room. She did a forward flip onto the mats. The cubs applauded. Except for Too-Tall.

"Stand up, Too-Tall!" barked Mr. Grizzmeyer. Too-Tall obeyed. But his knees were

OUR DEMONSTRATOR, MS. BLACK BELT BARR!

wobbling. Mr. Grizzmeyer went up to him. "For this demonstration I need three volunteers," said Mr. Grizzmeyer. He poked Too-Tall in the chest three times. "You, you, and you!"

Too-Tall's knees were shaking so hard they were a blur. "M-me, me, and me?" he cried.

Mr. Grizzmeyer grabbed Too-Tall by the arm and pulled him to the center of the

mats. Ms. Barr came forward and faced Too-Tall. Shaking, Too-Tall closed his eyes. Everyone else's eyes were on Ms. Barr. What would she do to the big bully who had tried so hard to break her? SHE might try to break HIM! In half, maybe!

But to the cubs' surprise, Ms. Barr didn't make a move at Too-Tall. In fact, she began talking. She talked about bullies and mean practical jokes. She talked about how everyone should try to get along with everyone else. As she spoke, Too-Tall found the courage to open his eyes again. And after a while, he even stopped shaking.

"All right, Too-Tall," said Ms. Barr finally. "You may sit down again." Too-Tall returned to his place. Then Ms. Barr chopped several boards in half, smashed a pile of bricks, and did a series of kicks and leaps. The cubs and other teachers clapped loudly.

"Okay, cubs," said Mr. Grizzmeyer. "Fun's over. Back to class."

The cubs walked down the hall toward Teacher Bob's classroom. The gang crowded around Too-Tall. "Boy, are you lucky, boss," said Skuzz. "Ms. Barr could have clobbered you!"

"You're right," said Too-Tall. He was still stunned. "How about that? She never even touched me!"

"And she never would," said Bertha Broom. "She's a grownup. She would never

hurt a cub. Not even a creep like you."

"Phew!" said Too-Tall.

"But I'm not a grownup," added Bertha. "And I might only be a brown belt. But I can tell you that if you play one more trick on Ms. Barr, I'll brown-belt you black-and-blue!"

And that was the last time Bertha ever had to mention karate to Too-Tall. Ms. Barr came back to class that afternoon. And although Too-Tall and his gang were not exactly angels for the rest of the week, they didn't play a single trick on the substitute teacher.

Stan and Jan Berenstain began writing and illustrating books for children in the early 1960s, when their two young sons were beginning to read. That marked the start of the best-selling Berenstain Bears series. Now, with more than 95 books in print, videos, television shows, and even Berenstain Bears attractions at major amusement parks, it's hard to tell where the Bears end and the Berenstains begin!

Stan and Jan make their home in Bucks County, Pennsylvania, near their sons—Leo, a writer, and Michael, an illustrator—who are helping them with Big Chapter Books stories and pictures. They plan on writing and illustrating many more books for children, especially for their four grandchildren, who keep them well in touch with the kids of today.